THE SMUGGLERS BOOK

POINT SPANIARD

ALAN SANDERS-CLARKE

HOLWILL PUBLICATIONS
71 The Green, Charlbury, Chipping Norton, OX7 3QB, UK
First published in 2020 by Holwill Publications
ISBN 978-0-9935569-7-5

Edited by Rachel Bladon
Designed by Rani Rai
Cover image by Kyle Richardson
Cover model Colin Guard
Back cover logo by Fishboy PZ

First Edition

www.thesmugglersofmousehole.com

For Helen, Rachel and Michele

Books in this children's series:

The Skull Rock Mystery

The Cave of Secrets

The Race to La Morna

The Search for the Crystal Skulls

The Mooncircle

Point Spaniard

Merlin's Temple (coming soon)

Other books for adults by the author:

Gallows Tree Hall (coming soon)

Cornish Short Stories (coming soon)

In memory of

Reverend Julyan Drew

A note from the author

As I put the finishing touches to this book, I can't help but reflect on the humble beginnings of the *Smugglers of Mousehole* story, and the unexpected journey it has taken me on since the basic idea for it first came to me in 2015.

Back then, I simply had fun and allowed my imagination to run riot, and before long I had written a book. I intended to stop there, but it felt like the characters wouldn't let me. They had taken on lives of their own in my head, and they had so many things they wanted to do!

What I hadn't anticipated was these characters would in turn inhabit other people's heads, and fire their imagination in completely different ways.

In 2016, Kyle Richardson, who had been inspired by reading the first book, asked to use it as a basis for a modern dance performance. I was blown away by this suggestion, yet his idea soon expanded into an even more ambitious project: a local community collaboration in which scores of volunteers, including many children, created a short *Smugglers of Mousehole* film. The team work, dedication and end results were amazing.

Fast forward three years and we have now secured British Film Institute funding to develop the story into a possible TV series. I am so proud, and excited about where my characters have led us, and how they continue to grow, expand and, hopefully, inspire.

With best wishes,

Alan Sanders-Clarke

CONTENTS

———◆———

Mousehole

In the year 1766

1

A GOOD HAUL

A distant gunshot broke the still of the morning and Joey and Dorcas, who had been rowing slowly along in the cold early-spring sun, both started.

'Gamekeeper, I expect,' said Joey. He handed the oars to Dorcas, reached down into the water to haul up the first lobster pot of the day, and grinned. It was filled with several dark brown lobsters that scrabbled with each other against the sides of the basket.

As Dorcas rowed them on from one pot to the next, Joey lifted each one out of the water with a little shout of joy. It was a good haul, and he held each of the baskets up to show Dorcas before stowing them carefully at the front of the boat.

He and Dorcas had been friends since they were very young. Her father Solomon Queach, the landlord of the Three Pilchards Tavern, was a friend of his own father James Trewidden. For years, Dorcas and Joey had tumbled about together on the beaches of this part of the Cornish coast, running like tearaways across the sand, scavenging in the rockpools and diving under the surf.

Both fourteen now, they had each started to take on more work for their families, Dorcas helping her mother in the kitchen of the Three Pilchards, and Joey sorting the catch after his father's fishing excursions, and overseeing the lobster pots. Joey often helped Solomon Queach to unpack the barrels of ale that were carted over to the Three Pilchards from Penzance – and in return, Dorcas came out when she could to help him bring in the lobsters.

'Hey, what's that, up on Point Spaniard?' said Dorcas, tilting her head and shaking her brown hair back from her face as she looked up. Joey followed her gaze, and saw a flash of bright sunlight bounce back from high up on the hillside. The light angled, then disappeared, and the two of them then made out the distant shape of a man who had something raised to his head.

'I think he's got a telescope!' said Joey. 'I wonder who it is. Was he looking at us?'

'Well, I don't think so. But if he was, he won't see us down here,' said Dorcas. They were a little closer to the shore now, and the overhang of the cliff was probably hiding most of the boat from view.

As they watched, the man threw something long and narrow down into the deep mass of yellow gorse bushes beneath the point where he was standing. 'Did he just throw the telescope away?' Dorcas said.

'Don't know,' said Joey. 'But we're getting a bit too close to the rocks!' There was a brisk onshore wind, and while they'd been watching the man, their boat had drifted still closer towards the shore, and they were now being pulled towards a tall rock that protruded up from the water like a huge crooked finger.

14

Joey took up the oars and began rowing rapidly back out to sea. His mind was focused on the currents now, but Dorcas was still peering up at the hillside, puzzled.

'Look! He's running away!' Dorcas said. 'There's only one person who runs like that. It's got to be Jonah Gollop!'

'Lolloping Gollop?' said Joey. 'What's he doing wandering about up on Point Spaniard?'

Gollop was a tall ungainly figure who, with his long legs, big hands and feet and awkward gait, had of course acquired the nickname 'Lolloping Gollop' in his home village of Mousehole. He was generally very busy as a junior clerk working in the mayor's office in Penzance. He was seldom to be seen out and about in Mousehole, even now when he had very little to do because the mayor, Edward Pentreath, was in Truro prison, awaiting trial for suspected murder.

'He'll be up to no good, you can be sure,' Joey went on, 'if he's anything like his master, that is. Anyway, it's your turn with the oars, Dorcas. We've got to get this haul ashore before the morning market starts!'

2

The customs men

It felt good to pull into Mousehole harbour with the lobster pots laden, and Joey was pleased with himself. Although his father was, he hoped, about to come into a big inheritance, everything depended on the court case involving Edward Pentreath. That was several weeks away, though, and Joey knew that money was already tight at home, and all the preparations to fight their case had made things even worse.

With Dorcas's help, he started to unload the catch onto the wharf, just down from the Salty Dog tavern. Just then a long low whistle attracted their attention, and looking up they saw Duncan, a close friend of both their fathers, walking along the wharf towards them.

'James will be pleased when he sees this little lot,' said Duncan, ruffling Joey's hair. 'Hopefully that'll take him out of the sour mood he's in this morning!'

'You've been with him, then?' said Joey.

'I have,' said Duncan. 'We've been up at Kemyel Manor, looking at all the work that will need doing when you take possession of the place.'

'*If* we take possession,' said Joey. 'Father's on edge and sure that something will go wrong at the trial. Or that it will all turn out to be a dream!'

Joey's father had discovered three months earlier that he was not the humble fisherman's orphan he'd always believed, but in fact the heir to the Penrose family estate, and the grand but crumbling old manor house of Kemyel. Thanks to the treachery of Edward Pentreath, James's parents had drowned at sea when he was just a baby. He had then been raised by a local woman known to him as 'Aunt Rachel', who herself had never really known the truth about the child that she had cared for as if he were her own.

'Well,' Duncan said, 'it's bound to feel strange, and difficult to believe. But I've known your father since he was a lad, and I can tell you, I'm not surprised at all to find out he's aristocracy. There's always been something special about James …' He rubbed the grey stubble on his chin thoughtfully, then grinned and added, 'And you only have to look at the way he likes to lord it over us all!' The playful expression on his face changed suddenly as he glanced over Joey's shoulder and caught sight of a group of people further up the wharf. He frowned and said, 'Mmm. This looks like trouble.'

Joey and Dorcas followed his gaze. There were four men in the group, and they were led by a short, stocky man in a stiffly starched black jacket, who had small round glasses perched on the end of his nose and was waving around a document officiously. He was pointing out across the harbour, and the other men who followed him, who were all smartly dressed, nodded enthusiastically at everything he said, with the air of men who would have nodded regardless of what they heard.

'Who are they?' asked Joey.

'It'll be the customs men,' said Duncan. 'I heard in the Three Pilchards last night that they've appointed a new captain, to root out every bit of smuggling in the area – and sure as day is day, that'll be him. You wait – it'll blacken your father's mood again when he hears he and his men have turned up in Mousehole already.'

3

HECTOR SNIPE

It had been a great honour for Hector Snipe to learn that he had been appointed captain in charge of His Majesties Customs, based in Penzance.

The letter from Sir Rupert Fox-Carne, the Lord Lieutenant of Cornwall, had referred to some difficulty the office in Penzance had had filling the role 'due to the unwillingness of those who abide thereabouts to take up the position'. There had been a significant increase in free trading in the area around Mousehole, the letter had gone on to say, and Snipe's task was to do 'whatever necessary' to stamp out smuggling in the community.

Hector Snipe had no qualms at all about doing 'whatever necessary'. He prided himself on being a man of his word, who would stop at nothing to get the results he wanted, in any situation. He viewed smuggling in particular as a scourge on society that needed to be excised, like a boil. No sooner had he arrived in Penzance than he began putting together a group of young officers to support him in his work.

This was their first visit to Mousehole, and Snipe had asked his clerk, Norris Jones, to take detailed notes about the geography of the area while they were there. The village was quiet that day, but as they made their way along the wharf, Snipe noticed a couple of grubby urchin children unloading lobster pots from a rowing boat. A tall grey-haired man was standing with them, and there was a slight sneer on his face as the group walked past. 'He's one of them for sure: just the sort of miscreant we'll be looking for,' Snipe thought to himself. Many of the men of this village were known as troublemakers, but he would root them out, one and all, of that everybody could be certain. Captain Snipe knew that his new job would quite possibly make him the most despised man in the district – but that kind of concern had never worried a man like him.

Captain Snipe was well versed in the tricks of the trade for tackling smuggling, but having moved from Exeter to Penzance to take up his new appointment, he was unfamiliar with the area itself. He would certainly need to engage the help of one or two locals who could update him on the comings and goings of key people in the area, and on general gossip. He'd been left the papers of Captain Wylde, the previous man in this role, who was now serving time in Bodmin Gaol for taking a personal share of every smuggling run he'd intercepted. Snipe had tutted to himself disapprovingly as he flipped through the man's papers, at the appalling thought of someone using his position of responsibility for personal gain. However, there were a couple of useful suggestions among the notes for local people Wylde had used as informants.

Back in Penzance, once Captain Snipe and his men had made a detailed survey of the coast and possible landing points around Mousehole, the captain went in search of the two people Wylde had mentioned. The first name, 'Jacob the Pedlar', drew a blank: the man had fled

Cornwall some months ago, a woman in the street told him when he asked, and no one had seen or heard of him since. Cautiously picking a different person to ask about the second possible informant, though, Snipe got better luck. The beggar 'Scratchface' Trudgeon would almost certainly be found in Chapel Street, a delivery boy told him. 'Near the Blind Fiddler,' he added.

Snipe set off from his office in the harbour, walking up Abbey slip to Chapel Street and turning right towards the town centre. He had thought that 'the Blind Fiddler' might be the name of an inn, but realised quickly that it was in fact a street busker who stood on the corner scraping away at his violin. Just as the boy had said, seated on the gravel path just a few feet away from the Blind Fiddler was none other than the beggar 'Scratchface' Trudgeon. Scratchface was so-named because of the three scars that ran across his left cheek from ear to nose. A strange-looking man, he was thin and slightly hunched, with several missing teeth. He looked like someone of greatly advanced years, yet his jet-black hair and sharp beady eyes belied a man who was younger than many believed. Cleverly, he always made a point of placing himself near the Blind Fiddler because anyone from outside town would naturally assume he was collecting on the busker's behalf and would throw the odd groat into his upturned cap, completely unnoticed by the Blind Fiddler nearby.

Snipe knew better than to be caught speaking directly to Trudgeon, so he waited until the street was completely clear of passers-by, and then took the opportunity to walk past and hiss at the beggar, 'St. Mary's Chapel in five minutes. Make sure you're not followed. I'll be waiting for you behind the ancient yew tree.'

Snipe had read in Wylde's detailed notes that this had been a regular meeting point for himself and Trudgeon. Heading back down Chapel Street he quickly spotted the old wooden spire of the chapel at the bottom of the hill, and it was easy to identify the great old yew tree, which was tucked away in the graveyard, its huge canopy providing a secluded spot where no conversation could easily be overheard.

He had only been waiting beneath the tree for a couple of minutes when he heard a scuffle in the bushes, and the beggar Trudgeon appeared warily, clutching his heavy ragged coat around him and keeping a few paces away.

'You helped Captain Wylde for some time in his work I understand,' Snipe said. 'I have recently taken over his position as captain in charge of His Majesty's Customs and Excise in Penzance.

'I'm here because there's been a big increase in smuggling in this area, in particular in Mousehole, and it is my task to eradicate these activities. Penzance is not a large place, and I need to know exactly what is happening here. People's comings and goings, you could say.

'Of course, it goes without saying that any conversations between us shall be in the *strictest* confidence, but if you work closely with me, I assure you that your contribution will be well rewarded.

'I will need you to report back to me at this very spot at three o'clock every other afternoon, and you must take the utmost care not to be observed by anyone. You will *never* come to this meeting place without some sort of information, however small or incidental it might seem. I need to know as much as possible in order to piece together a picture of this district's activities, so that I can carry out my operation swiftly.'

With that, Snipe handed a crown to the beggar, who turned it over in his hand. It was a generous amount, and for a regular installment like that he would happily seek out any information he could lay his hands on.

'Thursday afternoon at three, then,' said Snipe, as he turned heel and headed back towards town, leaving Scratchface Trudgeon to ponder this new opportunity that had opened up for him.

'Nice,' he said quietly to himself as he leaned against the trunk of the ancient yew tree. 'Very nice indeed.'

4

BAD NEWS

The following morning, in the early morning light, James had taken a long slow walk up to Kemyel Manor, as he had done often over the past couple of months. Discovering about his birthright had been overwhelming at first, and still when he stood at the great gate that marked the end of the driveway to the manor, he could not quite believe that this was where he had been born, and where his parents had lived.

He pushed the gate open and began to walk up to the front of the house, but was interrupted by the sound of galloping hooves behind him on the long gravel track that led to the manor from Raginnis.

The horseman was red in the face from riding fast, but as he pulled up at the gate and slipped from the saddle, James instantly recognised him as an acquaintance that he'd known since childhood.

'Why, if it isn't my old friend Josiah Sprout,' he said with a warm smile. 'What brings you up here to Kemyel so early in the morning?'

'Bad news, I'm afraid,' said Sprout. 'Very bad. Barnaby Coote was found dead on the floor of his cottage late yesterday evening. I've just been to identify his body at Archibald Screech's funeral parlour in Penzance.'

James Trewidden's face fell. He had only known Barnaby Coote well for a short time, but the man's bravery had helped him to bring Mayor Edward Pentreath to justice. He was the only person alive who had witnessed first hand Pentreath's men dispatching James's parents, the Penroses, many years before.

'That's not all,' said Sprout. 'He'd been shot. Word in Lamorna this morning is how convenient it is for Edward Pentreath to have him out of the way before the trial. He was your key witness, wasn't he?'

James Trewidden looked at Sprout, ashen-faced. 'He and my aunt Rachel,' he said, darkly. 'Has anyone seen her since yesterday?'

'Not that I know of,' said Sprout.

'Father!' called a voice, and turning, the two men saw Joey making his way towards them.

'Hello, Mr Sprout,' said Joey. 'Father, your mended nets are ready, and need to be picked up.'

'I'm sorry, son. I can't do that right now,' said James. 'Josiah here has just brought the news that Barnaby Coote has been shot dead, and I'm worried that Aunt Rachel may be in great danger. I need to get there straight away.'

Joey stopped in his tracks, and his mouth fell open. 'Shot dead?' he repeated, struggling to get his head around the news. 'But when? Where?'

'He was found yesterday evening at his cottage,' said Josiah Sprout.

'And if someone wants to get him out of the way, there's every reason they'll want Rachel out of the way too,' said James. 'I'm going to go up to Lamorna now.'

'I'll come with you,' said Joey.

'I'm sorry to bring bad news,' said Josiah Sprout. 'I do hope you'll find your aunt Rachel safe and well.' And he watched as James and his son marched off quickly along the path towards Lamorna.

The granite cottage was quiet as Joey and James approached, and there was no sign of Rachel in the little quillet outside, even though there was a thin warmth in the sun for probably the first time that year. Rachel was normally to be found tending to her beloved plants and vegetables for at least part of the day whatever the weather, and on a fine day she was often outside from daybreak until late in the afternoon. When they tapped at the door, there was no sound from inside, and when James tentatively turned the handle and went in, it was obvious from the silence that no one was at home.

'Let's look upstairs,' said Joey, starting up the crooked narrow staircase.

'No,' said James firmly, resting his hand on Joey's arm and looking him straight in the eyes, 'I'll go.'

James's tone sent a chill down Joey's spine: his father was afraid, he realised, of what they might find, and didn't want Joey to be the one to discover it. He waited in the front room, listening to the ticking of the carriage clock Rachel kept on the mantlepiece, and hearing creaking up above as James moved from the first room of the little cottage to the second.

'She's not here,' said James, appearing at the top of the stairs at last. 'But there's something strange. The cupboards where she keeps her clothes are open, and there are shoes and coats lying on the floor. The bedcover has been pulled off too. Rachel *never* leaves her room like that – nothing is ever left out of place here normally.'

Joey frowned. It was true: in his memory, every time they'd visited Aunt Rachel, the little cottage had been neatly swept and tidy. Everything there had its place, and nothing was ever left lying on the sides or the table, as it was at their home in the rooms above the Salty Dog.

'Let's head into Lamorna,' said James, 'and find out if any of her friends have seen her.'

But there was no need; as they made their way out of the cottage, they saw Julie Treneer, one of Rachel's oldest friends, heading anxiously up the path.

'Young James!' she said. 'Is Rachel with you? Has something happened?'

'No,' said James. 'We're looking for her ourselves.'

Julie's shoulders slumped visibly. 'Oh,' she said. 'I did hope she might be with you. I'd said that I would call on her yesterday afternoon, but when I came, she wasn't here. I waited and waited, and in the end, I thought she must have been called away for something, and went home. I decided I'd come and check on her this morning, but as I was making my way over, I met Bert Truckle, who asked me where she was. She'd asked him to stop by late this morning to look at that hole in her roof, but when he arrived, she wasn't home.

'Oh James,' she went on. 'Where do you think she might be? I'm so worried, what with the awful thing that happened to Barnaby Coote.'

'I'm worried sick, too,' said James. 'That's why we came over here. And it looks to me as if someone may have been through her things. But let's try not to get too carried away. There could be a simple explanation. We need to think through all the places she might possibly have gone to.'

They did exactly that, but after three hours of searching, and asking at almost every house in Lamorna, they were none the wiser. All they were able to find out was that Rachel had last been seen early the previous morning, buying some milk from Castallack farm on the outskirts of the village. She'd seemed fine, the farmer assured James and Joey – very much her normal cheerful self – and she had been talking of how it felt as if the weather was warming up at last and she was looking forward to spending the next day in her quillet doing some planting.

5

JAMES MAKES A PLAN

Joey and James decided to go their separate ways from Lamorna – Joey heading back to Mousehole, where Rachel had many friends, and James to see Sir Rupert Fox-Carne at The Lookout – his grand townhouse in Penzance. Perhaps Fox-Carne would have more information about the murder of Barnaby Coote that might help to solve the mystery of Rachel's disappearance. Julie Treneer said that she would wait in Rachel's cottage until dusk, in case she came back, in which event she promised to send word to the Salty Dog.

Darkness had already fallen by the time James came home, and he looked tired and worn. Joey, who had had no luck asking around in Mousehole, fetched a drink for his father, and then sat down to listen as James shared the latest news with him and his concerned mother, Lizzie.

'It turns out they've already arrested someone for Coote's murder,' said James. 'A Herbert Gribble. Gribble owed Coote money, apparently, and he went to see him and things got nasty. Gribble says he acted in self-defence.'

'It's nothing to do with Pentreath or the trial?' said Lizzie.

'Apparently not,' said James.

'Well, that's a relief,' she said. 'Rachel must just have gone away suddenly, then, and forgotten to tell anyone.'

'Maybe,' said James, but he grimaced and shook his head. 'It just isn't like her though. To arrange things with people and then let them down.'

'You stop worrying about her, my love,' said Lizzie. 'Rachel's a strong woman, and she can take care of herself. I'm sure she'll be back in plenty of time for the trial.'

'That's the other problem,' said James. 'Sir Fox-Carne said that because of Coote's murder, the trial has been put back by another month. I'm afraid I'm going to have to do a trip to Roscoff.'

'Oh no, James,' said Lizzie. 'You know the customs people were all over Mousehole just the other day. We said there'd be no more smuggling trips. I'm sure we can make do and get through till the trial.'

'We can't, Lizzie,' said James, reaching an arm around her. 'Hopefully this will be the last one, and the Penrose estate will be ours in a couple of months. I'm sorry, but we won't be able to pay the rent on the inn otherwise. I've talked to the right people and I already have a loan set up to pay for the wares, and it'll give me enough profit to tide us over. But don't worry, it'll take that new customs captain a good while to catch on to us, and by the time he does, there'll be no more free trading for us Trewiddens!'

For many of the Mousehole families who struggled to make ends meet, even though it was illegal, smuggling was the only way of putting supper on the table each day. But because James and his friends were so generous with their booty, always sharing it among the villagers, and never taking enough of the profit to become wealthy themselves, even those in Mousehole who disapproved of free trading had long turned a blind eye to their activities.

'I'll go in the next few days,' said James. 'The weather looks like it's turning stormy tomorrow, but as soon as it clears up, we'll be off. Saturday or Sunday, perhaps. I'm going up to the Three Pilchards now to talk about it with the men. Don't you worry, Lizzie. It'll all be fine.'

'Father,' said Joey. 'Let me come with you. I'm fourteen now, and I've been managing the lobster pots all on my own. I know I could help.'

For just a moment, James hesitated. Then he saw the look on Lizzie's face, and put his hand on Joey's arm. 'I'll need you to be our eyes and ears hereabouts Joey. Your mother would never forgive me if I set you on the path of free trading – and if anything was to happen to us … well … then you'd need to step up to become the man of the house, and the inn.'

Joey knew his father well enough to understand that there was no point arguing, but as he watched him head out into the darkness, he felt bitterly disappointed.

'Joey,' said his mother gently. 'Your time will come. You're made for better things than free trading. One day you're going to be the master of Kemyel Manor, and we've got to keep you safe for that.'

There was a solemn air among the group that gathered around the long wooden table in the Three Pilchards that evening. Solomon Queach had cleared the tavern of other customers, so they could talk privately, and all of them – Duncan, Francis, Tobias Cass, Tim Newman, Gabriel Madron, and Solomon – listened silently and intently as James began to talk.

'As you know, I'd hoped I'd done my last free trading run some time ago,' he began, 'but Pentreath's trial has been delayed again, and it will now be much longer before I have access to Kemyel Manor, and the rightful inheritance of my parents. Times have been hard these last few months, as we all know, and I can't wait longer for income. I've arranged a loan to pay for a big haul of brandy from Roscoff and I'm hoping that you can all join me to help bring it back.'

Solomon Queach took a long sip of ale, and then said, 'James, I too could do with some money, times really have been so hard of late. But with all this activity going on in Penzance, are we not playing into the customs people's hands? If we're caught it would mean the hangman's noose for the lot of us.'

'That's why I want to go sooner rather than later,' said James. 'Saturday, or Sunday at the latest. That man Snipe has been out here doing surveys, but it's unlikely he'll have caught on to us just yet. I've planned it carefully in my mind. We'll pick the booty up from François-Xavier on the Ile de Batz, well away from prying eyes, then bring it back to Porthgwarra, not the caves near Mousehole.

There'll be less chance of being caught over there in the far west, where there are so few customs patrols.'

'Well, I'm in,' said Tobias Cass at once. He had no family to worry about at home and was always the first to volunteer for a smuggling run. There was a pause and glances around the table before Francis, Tim, Gabriel and Duncan put themselves forward too.

'I can't do it,' said Solomon, awkwardly. 'I'm sorry, James. I promised my wife, and she'll not forgive me this time.'

James put his hand on Solomon's shoulder. 'I understand, Sol. It's a hard decision for all of us.'

They were a close-knit bunch, and knew and trusted each other implicitly. It was also a trip they'd done on many occasions in the past – but even so there was a definite air of uneasiness about this particular run that each man felt keenly. They were all conscious of the appearance in Mousehole of Snipe's new customs team, and none of them quite shared James's confidence that he was not yet ready to take action against them.

6

SNIPE SEEKS INFORMATION

As James had predicted, Thursday had dawned a dreadful day, with great squalls of rain hammering the southern coast of Cornwall. The Blind Fiddler had waited until nearly midday before settling himself on Chapel Street in Penzance, where he was sheltered from the rain by the overhanging roof of the Union Hotel. The beggar Scratchface was later than usual installing himself alongside too, and once he had huddled in the dry and leant his head against the wall, he quickly dozed off. When the town hall clock struck three, he was still snoring soundly – but at the sound of the third stroke, he leapt to his feet, and set off sprinting down the hill towards St. Mary's Chapel. The Blind Fiddler was aware of him leaving, and after finishing his tune, he tucked his fiddle under one arm and tapped his way quietly down the street.

Luckily for Trudgeon, Snipe had been waylaid with some business in the office, and was also late arriving for their assignment under the yew tree. 'Well?' he demanded as he dipped under its huge branches to shelter from the rain. 'What do you have for me?'

'Not a lot today, Cap'n, what with the weather being so filthy and all,' said Trudgeon. 'I've been keepin' my eyes and ears to the ground though,' he added hastily, noticing the look of distrust pass across Hector Snipe's face. 'There ain't a lot that gets past old Scratchface here!'

'Well, that's not good enough, Trudgeon,' Snipe said sharply. 'If you can't find a little more for me than that, I'll have to look elsewhere for my information.'

'Oh now, now,' said Trudgeon anxiously. 'It's groundwork that's needed first, see, Cap'n Snipe. That's what I've been doin' these two days, groundwork. Like puttin' out all your nets when you're at sea. Gotta get 'em all out first and leave 'em for a bit, before you can start reelin' them in. See what I'm sayin', Cap'n?'

Snipe sighed. 'I'll give you one more chance,' he said. 'I'll meet you here on Monday at three. Make sure you have something for me then.'

'Ah,' said Trudgeon, 'there's jus' one little problem with that, Cap'n Snipe, sir. Only this groundwork I'm doin', like I said, it's costing me a fair penny. I might need a little … a little extra funding, shall we say, jus' to get things started, like.'

Snipe frowned, wavering for a moment, then he took a half-crown from his pocket and tossed it across to Trudgeon. 'You'd better have something good for me by Monday,' he said. 'Really good.'

'Oh, I will, Cap'n Snipe, sir,' said Trudgeon. 'You can rest assured o' that.'

Snipe put up his collar and darted back out from the cover of the tree into the rain; Trudgeon, waiting for a moment or two until the captain had turned out of the churchyard, then followed. The rain drenched his ragged old coat in no time, but the feel of the shiny coin in his fingers warmed him to the core. There was no need for him to go back to his cold, wet station in Chapel Street now: he'd made in a few minutes what it normally took him a week or more to collect in his beggar's dish. No, what was needed now was some thinking time, and a plan for how to get some information for that man Snipe. And what better place for thinking than in front of the fire in one of Penzance's finest inns – the Turk's Head. Who knew, maybe there was even information to be had there too.

An hour later, as Scratchface Trudgeon ordered his second jar of ale, the Blind Fiddler, still in his spot on Chapel Street scratching away at his tunes, heard what he'd been listening out for. The light-footed step approached, and then stopped, and there was a pause as the person fumbled in a small shoulder bag. The same thing happened every week in the afternoons, twice, like clockwork, when Dorcas Queach made her way home to Mousehole after taking lunch for her elderly grandmother in Penzance. 'There you are, sir,' said her gentle young voice, as a coin clattered into the fiddler's chipped collection plate.

'Miss Queach, that be?' whispered the fiddler, tucking his violin under his elbow and reaching out for her arm with his hand.

'Yes, sir, it's me, Dorcas,' came the reply.

'You tell your father to be careful,' said the fiddler, quietly. 'There's folks asking questions about free-trading in these parts, and there's some that don't mind tellin' them all about it. You tell 'im that from me.'

And with that, he took up his fiddle again and started playing where he had left off, lost in his music, so that to all the world it looked as if he had just stopped to thank the girl for her donation. She frowned, anxiously, then hurried on down the street towards the coastal path.

7

A WARNING FOR JAMES

It was quiet in the Salty Dog when Solomon Queach and his daughter Dorcas came in, their hair straggled and wet from the wind and the rain outside. A couple of old fishermen were drinking in the corner, and Joey was sweeping the floor while Lizzie sat flicking through the book where she wrote down the family's outgoings and income for the week.

'Why, if it isn't Mr Solomon Queach and his lovely daughter!' she said, looking up with a smile. 'Come in out of that awful weather and have a drink.'

'It is a foul one out there indeed,' said Solomon, taking a seat at Lizzie's table. 'I'm mighty glad not to be out on the water in this.'

'Joey, fetch Solomon a cup of ale, and you two young folk – get yourselves something too,' said Lizzie. 'James is not here, I'm afraid, Sol. He's been over in Lamorna since this afternoon, looking for Rachel and seeing what he can find out. He can't stop worrying about her.'

'Still no news then?' said Solomon.

'Not a word. Of course, now we know that poor old Barnaby Coote's death was nothing to do with the trial, I've told him he's really no need to worry. I'm sure she's just gone away to see family and forgotten to tell him, but it's thrown him into a terrible dark mood.' She lowered her voice. 'That and worrying about this trip to Roscoff.'

'That's why we've come,' said Solomon, quietly. 'I wanted to speak to him about it, but in all honesty it's probably better if I speak to you instead. I know what James is like when he's made up his mind about something, and you probably have a better chance than anyone of talking him round. Dorcas here was warned off this afternoon, by the Blind Fiddler in Penzance.'

Dorcas and Joey, bringing drinks, slid onto the bench at the table. 'That's right, Lizzie,' said Dorcas. 'He said someone's been asking questions – that Hector Snipe, I suppose – and someone's giving him the information he needs. I think he might mean the beggar, Scratchface Trudgeon. He was always selling information to Captain Wylde, and I suppose he's doing the same thing again.'

Lizzie sighed. 'That *is* bad news – but it'll not stop my James. You know him, like you say, Sol. I've tried everything already to warn him not to make this trip, but he won't change his mind. I've got a bad feeling about it, and this makes me even more sure it's a bad idea. But he's got the loan now, and I know there's no going back on it.'

'Well, he really ought to think twice about it,' said Solomon. 'It sounds like that Snipe character has got his feet under the desk a little faster than we'd thought.'

'Well, I'll speak to him again tonight, Sol,' said Lizzie. 'But like I say, I really don't hold out much hope of him changing his mind.'

'When was he planning on leaving?'

'Sunday at first light, he said to me,' said Joey. 'The weather's still bad tomorrow but looks set to ease off by Saturday – and Gabriel Madron wanted to wait a day for the water to settle.'

'Two days out, and three days back, with the winds blowing as they are,' said Solomon. 'They should be back late Thursday.'

Lizzie sighed. 'I've got a bad feeling in my bones about it and I'll be mighty relieved when it's all over. And this will be the last one, he promises me, as long as everything goes well with the trial.'

The four of them sat chatting for a while, but Joey was quiet and thoughtful. When Solomon and Dorcas got up to go, he put on his coat as well.

'I'm just going over to Francis' cottage, Mother,' he said. 'Dorcas, will you come with me? There's something I want to ask him.'

'Of course,' said Dorcas. 'Thank you for the drink, Lizzie. And please tell James to mind himself.'

'I will, Dorcas,' said Lizzie. 'And thank you for bringing us that news so quickly.'

Grabbing his coat, Joey followed Solomon and Dorcas out of the Salty Dog, then shook Solomon's hand and turned with Dorcas up the Gurnick.

'What is it, Joey?' asked Dorcas. 'What did you want to see Francis about?'

'I just had an idea, while we were sitting talking. Everyone seems to think that the crew shouldn't make this run, and I know it's getting Mother really worried. But she's right: my father won't listen to anyone, and he's made up his mind to go. I feel like I need to stand up for her, so I was just wondering if I can help somehow and this idea suddenly came to me. It's … it's quite a big plan, but with your help, and Francis's, I think it might work.'

They had reached Francis's little low-slung cottage, which sat perched up at the far end of Mousehole, looking across to St Clement's Isle. Joey knocked on the newly-painted grey front door, and his eyes were sparkling slightly as he looked at Dorcas. 'Let's see what you both think,' he said, 'and if you'd be prepared to help.'

8

JOEY STAYS AWAY

'When did you say Joey will be back?' James asked Lizzie. It was Friday lunchtime, and his head was spinning. As well as worrying about Rachel, he had a hundred different things to do to get ready for his departure on Sunday, and he was used to relying on Joey to help him when he was busy. But that morning, Joey had declared that he was going up to his Aunt Sarah's cottage in Raginnis for a few days, to shore up her roof as slates had come off and a rafter needed replacing. He said that he'd be staying overnight too, at least until the weather passed and he'd got the cottage properly back in the dry.

'Didn't say,' said Lizzie, tight-lipped. 'But he probably won't be back before Monday.'

James sighed. Lizzie had spent the night before trying to persuade him not to make the trip to Roscoff, and he knew that she was very unhappy about it all. Presumably that was why Joey had made himself scarce too. The day had not started well: Francis had pulled out of the trip, saying something had come up that he couldn't put off, but refusing to say more. That meant taking two boats to Roscoff, as Francis was the only one with a lugger big enough to carry the entire load back. Lizzie had told him that Joey had been at Francis's cottage just the evening before and James now began to wonder … was Joey deliberately trying to talk his friends out of the trip?

'You don't know what he was talking about with Francis last night, do you?' James asked Lizzie. 'It's so unlike Francis to let me down at the last minute.'

'Perhaps he realises what a foolhardy idea it is,' said Lizzie, tersely.

'Come on, Lizzie,' said James softly, putting his arm around her shoulders. 'You know I wouldn't go if I didn't have to. But what with the court case being postponed, I really don't have any choice.'

'We'd find a way to manage, James, you know we would,' said Lizzie with a frustrated sigh.

'It's the last one. I've promised you that, and I'll keep my word. I'll be back on Thursday night, and that will be the end of my free trading days, like I said.'

The door of the Salty Dog opened, and the hulking figure of Tim Newman appeared in the doorway.

'Weather's starting to turn at last, James,' he said. 'I'm all set for Sunday, but I'm off up-country till tomorrow evening, so I just came to let you know that. We've lost Francis, I hear?'

'Yes,' said James. 'No one else though, do you know?'

'No, all good,' said Tim. 'I've just seen the rest of them up at the Three Pilchards, and we're all set.'

James breathed a sigh of relief. If he'd been more than one man down, he'd have been starting to worry, but with just

Francis missing, he was fairly confident things should go as planned.

'That's good news, Tim. Are you happy for us to take your boat, now we don't have the big lugger? We'll need two to get all the barrels back, and I thought my boat and yours are probably the most seaworthy at the moment, for a longer trip like that.'

'That's what we said too,' said Tim. 'I've been down at the harbour this morning checking her over, and she's all set.'

'That's good,' he said, shaking Tim's hand. 'Thank you, Tim. Sunday at six, then?'

'Sunday at six.'

9

A CHANCE ENCOUNTER

James spent the rest of Friday, and Saturday, getting his own boat ready for the long trip across the Channel, and without Joey to help out, he was rushed off his feet and barely at home to face Lizzie's disapproval. But when he got up in the dark very early on Sunday morning, he found her already up, and dividing up a big pail of pottage that she'd made to keep the two crews going on their long journey.

'You be careful, James Trewidden,' she said, with tears in her eyes, as he gathered his things and pulled on his oilskins. 'You come back to me safe and sound.'

James wrapped her in his arms and held her tightly for a moment or two. 'I will, Lizzie, I will. Don't you worry.'

She watched from the door of the Salty Dog as he headed down to the harbour at sunrise to meet his faithful crewmen. Then she turned away, wiping her eyes, and busied herself sweeping, polishing and tidying in the inn. It was going to be a long few days, she knew.

It was seven by the time the two boats were heading quietly out of the harbour, and after a still day on Saturday, the sea was calm. The sun had risen to reveal a perfect spring sky, its bright blue broken by just a few scudding clouds.

Many of the villagers who were up and about by that time saw the two boats leave, but said nothing, commenting to each other only on the turn in the weather.

Casper Sloth, setting off early to spend the day and evening in Penzance with his colleagues from the mayor's office, had also spotted the boats. Their small shapes were still visible on the horizon as he rounded the headland at Penlee Point and saw the familiar figure of Jim Bates, landlord of The Fisherman's Arms, leaning against an old tree between Mousehole and his tavern just half a mile further on, gazing out to sea.

'Mornin', young Mr Sloth. 'Certainly a better day to be out there today,' said Bates, nodding at the boats.

'Hmm,' said Sloth. 'They must be desperate to get some fishing in; it's not often you see anyone going out on a Sunday.'

Jim Bates stared back at him with a knowing look on his face and said, 'C'mon lad, you're a Mousehole boy, you know the score. Sure, they are off to sea, but this ain't no fishin' trip. James and his crew will be gone for a good few days. But o' course,' he added, tapping the bark of the tree he'd been leaning against, 'that's between you, me and this 'ere tree.'

'Of course,' said Sloth, looking surprised. Then, looking left and right as if to check that they were all alone, he said, 'Isn't it a bit risky with that new Captain doing the rounds?'

Bates mimicked Sloth, looking left to right before answering, 'Tis not an issue if you return in the dead of night far enough west of here, beyond the point where the customs men patrol.' Then he winked, tapped the side of his nose with his forefinger and put it to his lips, saying 'Shhh' in a low whisper.

Sloth nodded, returned the knowing look, and with a 'Good day' he continued on towards Penzance. How strange, he thought, as Jim Bates wasn't usually that talkative, as they didn't have that much in common. But he'd smelt ale on the landlord's breath, and wondered whether he'd still been drunk from the night before. In any case, this would give him something interesting to share with his colleagues when he saw them, he thought to himself. He would never dream of informing on the Mousehole men to Captain Snipe's office, of course, but it was always enjoyable to be the first one to know about goings-on in the neighbourhood, and to be able to surprise people with local 'secrets'.

10

TRUDGEON DOES SOME DIGGING

Scratchface Trudgeon had enjoyed drinking his way around the taverns of Penzance for three nights, feeling positively rich with the money given to him by Captain Snipe. He'd gone out each evening intending to dig for information about Mousehole's free trading, but had invariably bumped into old drinking friends and each time had found himself back home at the end of the night none the wiser and considerably worse for wear.

By Sunday evening, his money had almost run dry, and as he sat nursing his last pint of ale in the Admiral Benbow, he finally turned his mind to the problem of how to get hold of some information for Captain Snipe by the next afternoon. He had intended to get over to Mousehole for the evening, in the hopes of picking up any snippets in the taverns there, but it was a good hour's walk, and his legs ached from his days sitting out in the cold. Anyway, he told himself, there was always tomorrow morning.

But Trudgeon's luck was in that evening. As he reached the bottom of his pint, he saw the door of the tavern open, and in walked a group of the mayor's clerks, including Casper Sloth, who Trudgeon knew came from Mousehole, and who was renowned for his loose tongue. The group had clearly been drinking somewhere else already, and they made their way over to a large table by the fire and called loudly for some drinks. Trudgeon waited for a few minutes for them to settle down, and then he wandered casually over to their table.

'Evening gentlemen, would you mind if I warmed myself a little next to this cosy fire for a moment or two, then I'll be off out of your way.'

He was well known by the clerks, who passed him each day as they walked home from the mayor's office.

'Scratchface!' one of them called tipsily. 'I hope you're not planning to beg for a drink?' One or two of the other men laughed.

'Not at all,' replied Trudgeon, raising his glass to show that he already had one. 'I've 'ad a good day so thought I might celebrate by buyin' myself a pint of ale.'

He shuffled around the table to position himself as close as possible to Sloth, who was swaying around in his seat, and asked, 'So, 'ow's life in dear old Mousehole, Mr Sloth?'

'Well now Scratchface, you know Mousehole,' said Sloth with a big wink, and then a belch, which set his friends cackling with delight.

'I imagine the locals are strugglin' a bit. There can't be much fishin' going on in this 'ere weather we've been having,' Trudgeon went on.

'Funnily enough,' said Sloth, slurring his words, 'I just saw a couple of boats heading out today. They make them tougher in Mousehole, you see!' His friends laughed, and Casper Sloth, enjoying the attention, continued in ridiculously loud whisper, winking his eye again, 'Mind you, according to Jim Bates they'll be coming back with quite a load, as I was telling these fellows earlier.'

'Whooaa!' cried Sloth's friends, banging the sturdy wooden table in delight.

'Oh aye?' said Trudgeon, feigning ignorance. 'How's that then, Mr Sloth?'

The group laughed again, and one of Sloth's friends leaned in towards Trudgeon. 'Smugglin', Scratchface! That's what it'll be.'

Trudgeon gave a shocked look. 'What! But who on earth 'd be riskin' tha' with all them customs folk crawlin' all over the place?'

Everyone looked to Sloth. 'Well now,' he said. 'That'll be …' He hiccupped, and his friends laughed once more. 'Trewidden, James Trewidden and his crew!' he said, and then slumped with his head on the table.

'His crew?' said Trudgeon. 'An' who might be his crew?'

But Sloth was out for the count, and there was no response to be had, either from him or his giggling colleagues.

'Well, Mr Sloth, you look like you'll be needin' your bed,' said Trudgeon, and he finished the last dregs of his drink and put his glass down on the table with a sigh of satisfaction. 'An' I mine, too. Thank you kindly, gentlemen, for lettin' a poor soul warm himself in front of the fire. I'll be wishin' you a good night.'

And with that, Trudgeon, immensely satisfied with such a successful half-hour's work, wrapped his ragged coat a little tighter around his thin frame, and headed out into the night.

11

A VISIT TO MOUSEHOLE

It was very unlike Scratchface Trudgeon to be up and about early, but knowing that the ongoing arrangement with Captain Snipe was dependent on him getting hold of some solid information, he dragged himself out of bed on Monday morning, and by ten was walking down the hill from the small hamlet of Paul towards Mousehole.

He continued on through the village and to the wharf, where a number of fishermen were busily mending their nets. Having positioned himself close to one of them and sat quietly gazing out to sea for ten minutes or so, he attempted some small talk, but it was soon obvious that the old man was in no mood for conversation.

'I need to speak to one James Trewidden,' he said to the man. 'You wouldn't know where I might be findin' him, do you?'

The fisherman didn't answer, but a younger man nearby called out that Trewidden was away fishing for the next few days. 'You could go see 'is wife in the Salty Dog tavern if you wanted,' he added.

Scratchface thanked him, asked for some directions to the Salty Dog, and then headed off there. It was very warm and welcoming inside, and if Scratchface had had anything left of the money Snipe had given him, he would have loved nothing better than to settle down by the fire to sip on a pint of ale.

'Can I help you?' asked a round, rosy-cheeked woman at the bar, smiling warmly.

'I'm after James Trewidden,' Scratchface replied. 'I have a message for him from a friend in Penzance.'

'From Penzance?' said the woman eagerly. 'James is away fishing at present. But if it's about his aunt Rachel, I can pass on the message. We're all waiting for news of her.'

'No, it's a business matter, I'm afraid,' said Trudgeon. 'When might he be back, would you say?'

Lizzie, standing behind the bar, look at Trudgeon carefully. 'Who's askin'?' she said, a note of suspicion in her voice.

'Like I say, I've got business connections with Mr Trewidden an' the others,' said Trudgeon. 'Who's he gone with, if I might ask? So, I don't go lookin' for people who're away with 'im, you understand?'

'He's fishing with his fishing crew, like I say,' said Lizzie firmly. 'So, if as you say you have business connections with my James, you'll know where to look, I'm sure.'

Hearing the sharp note in Lizzie's voice, a few other people in the bar had looked up, and Trudgeon, conscious that he was treading on dangerous ground, did his best to grin confidently at Lizzie. ''Course I will!' he said. 'Thank you for your help, Mrs Trewidden.'

Trudgeon headed out of the Salty Dog and wandered back down to the harbour. Several of the fishermen looked up when they saw him walking back. They exchanged glances and then busied themselves with their work on the nets with the air of people who were not to be interrupted. There was a woman selling vegetables from a big basket at the far end of the harbour, and Trudgeon paused there for a few moments, pretending to admire the vegetables, and then sighing.

'Ar', I've come all the way from Penzance tryin' to make contact wi' the fisherman James Trewidden. I know he's out at sea, fishin' but I don't know how much longer for. You wouldn't know if he's gone alone, or if he's gone wi' someone, would you?'

The woman looked at Trudgeon suspiciously, and said, 'What's tha' go' to do wi' you or me? Now are you buyin' any vegetables, or jus' wastin' my time?'

The cloak of the village was pulled tight around the escapades of James Trewidden, that much was clear. There didn't appear to be anyone else out and about on the streets, and frustrated by his wasted journey, Trudgeon returned wearily towards the coast path that led back to Penzance via Newlyn. Just as he was leaving the village, he spotted another young man working away from the other fishermen, mending nets that were draped over the rocks beneath the path.

'Ow be?' he called, tentatively trying to gauge whether this was yet another suspicious villager.

The young man looked up from his work, smiled and replied, 'Ansum, thank ee.'

'I don't suppose you can 'elp me,' said Trudgeon, stepping off the path to come a little closer to the young man. 'I'm tryin' to get an urgent message to James Trewidden, bu' I know he's out fishin' an' his wife wasn't there when I called a' the Salty Dog. Do you know anyone who could get a message to 'im sharpish?'

The young man put down his net, wiped his brow with his hand and shook his head. ''Fraid I can't help ye,' he said, 'I'm thinkin' all those who could pass a message on are out at sea with 'im.'

'I thought as much,' said Trudgeon. 'Who might they be, so's I can keep an eye out for them when they come back? Jus' in case I can't get hold of Trewidden himself?'

'Ah, it's the usual crew,' said the young man, without hesitation. 'Duncan … that's Duncan Johns, Tobias Cass, Tim Newman and Gabriel Madron. Not Solomon Queach this time, I believe, an' I heard Francis has not joined them for this trip either.'

'So that's Duncan, Tobias Cass …'

'Tim and Gabriel,' said the fisherman.

'An' when would they be back in the village, would you say?' asked Trudgeon.

'Now there, I 'ave no idea,' said the young man. 'Next

weekend, perhaps? Anyway, I hope one of 'em can help you when they're back. Good day to you!'

'And to you too!' said Trudgeon, reciting the names in his head as he set off along the path, a spring in his step now that he at last had some useful information for Captain Snipe. He didn't know when the smugglers would be likely to return, but a slow and steady filter of information was better anyway for keeping those crowns coming, and now at least he had some names to pass on.

12

TRUDGEON REPORTS BACK

On the stroke of three o'clock that afternoon, Captain Hector Snipe ducked under the deep canopy of the old yew tree in St. Mary's Chapel graveyard, and found Scratchface Trudgeon already there waiting for him, with a smirk on his face.

'Well, what do you have for me?' snapped the captain.

'Some very interestin' news indeed,' said Trudgeon. 'Turns out a group of fishermen set out from Mousehole jus' yesterday mornin'. An' I have names for you.' He took out a torn old envelope from his pocket, on the back of which he'd written the names of James Trewidden and his crew.

The captain read the names, then looked askance at Trudgeon. 'Who's to say these men aren't just out on a fishing trip?' he asked. 'What makes you think otherwise?'

'Ah,' said Trudgeon, 'I have it from one of my many trusted sources.'

'Well, I'll need more information than this,' said Snipe. 'When are they due back? Where will they be coming in?'

'All in good time, Cap'n,' said Trudgeon. 'I don't wan' to be raisin' suspicions, by askin' too many questions all at once. But I dare say I can speak to my source once more, an' get a little more information for you.'

'You will indeed,' said Snipe. 'And bring it to me by tomorrow. Same time, same place.' He cast a couple of shillings into Trudgeon's hand, then turned, checked they were not being watched, and walked smartly back out into the churchyard.

13

THE ILE DE BATZ

It had stayed fine and dry for the journey across the channel to the Ile de Batz, just north of Roscoff, but by late Monday afternoon, as the sun tipped towards the horizon, rainclouds were beginning to gather. Tim Newman, who was on watch, looked up at them wondering how long it would be before the rain started to come down – and when he looked back across the water, he could make out the distant hazy line of land rising up above the horizon. He called out to the crews of the two boats that the Ile de Batz was visible up ahead, and there was a weary, relieved cheer. Lizzie's pottage had kept them all going strong, but it had been a long two days with no bed to rest in, and they were all ready to set food on land.

By the time they reached the island's small harbour, dusk was setting in, and the first spots of rain were starting to fall; but a strong-looking figure had come striding down to the quay to meet them, and they could see that there was already a stack of casks waiting under sack cloth: all signs that things were going as planned.

'Mr James!' called François-Xavier as they cast their ropes ashore. He was a balding, jovial Frenchman, and as he'd worked with James and his crew for many years, there were hugs, kisses and vigorous handshakes all round as he welcomed them onto dry land.

'We eat first, yes?' he asked. 'There is very little danger here. Come with me to our farm and we will have some wine, food and rest.'

'I think I'd prefer to load the boats first, François,' said James Trewidden.

'Well, yes, but why the hurry?' said François- Xavier.

'No hurry, I just want to get the job of carrying those casks out of the way before I relax and drink wine,' said James as he strode along the quayside, watched eagerly by his crew. He pulled back some of the sack cloth and said, '-I see you've done an excellent job of disguising them as I asked'. He reached down and rolled one of the barrels over to the men, so they could see for themselves the label PILCHARDS across the top, and feel the compact, solid feel of the contents. No hint at all of brandy glugging about inside.

'We'll taste the contents of this one before leaving, not only to confirm the very high quality of your brandy, François, but also to toast our friendship – and you will keep whatever is left in the keg from this evening as a small token of my appreciation.'

François- Xavier smiled, then set aside the keg to be taken to the farmhouse once the rest of the barrels had been loaded on board the boats.

It was fairly quick work between the six of them to pass the kegs across from one man on the quay to another on each of the boats, and to stow them carefully, but the men were already tired from their long journey, and by the time the boats were loaded up and they had crossed the three muddy fields that separated the quay from L'Escroc farmhouse, they all felt ready to collapse. They eagerly stepped into the old stone house, and the smell of the bubbling casserole that François-Xavier's wife Nerys had prepared for them filled the air. It made them realise that their hunger was even greater than their fatigue.

It was an evening full of laughter, as it always was at L'Escroc when James and his crew visited. They ate and drank, while François-Xavier's sons Georges and Gustav went and slept on the boats to protect their cargo, as they always did for the Mousehole men. Then, as Nerys cleared away the empty plates, François-Xavier rolled in the pilchard barrel that James had selected and prised off the lid, to reveal a smaller brandy keg inside.

'A small cup each and no more!' said James. 'We have a long journey ahead of us tomorrow and we need to keep our wits about us – but first a toast.' He raised his cup, and the men all followed. 'François-Xavier and his finest brandy!'

'François-Xavier and his finest brandy!' echoed the crew, raising their cups as well, bolting the amber nectar down and then sighing contentedly.

The brandy took effect on the tired, weather-worn men almost at once. The jollity of the evening had been fuelled by relief at arriving safely after this first leg of the expedition, but now their eyelids began to feel heavy, and the conversation slowly stilled. As they finished the last dregs of their drinks, François-Xavier rose and took a big pile of blankets from Nerys.

'Sleep now,' he said, laying the blankets on the floor in front of the fire. 'You will need your rest. And we will wake you with the first light.'

James shook his hand, then, like the others, wrapped himself in a blanket, and stretching himself out on the floor, was asleep in just a moment or two.

14

AT THE FISHERMAN'S ARMS

At about the same time that James took his first mouthful of Nerys's casserole on the Ile de Batz, across the Channel Scratchface Trudgeon was stepping into the Fisherman's Arms in Newlyn, and taking his place at the bar there. Casper Sloth had mentioned that it was Jim Bates, the inn's landlord, who'd told him about James Trewidden and the other smugglers, so Trudgeon had walked out to Newlyn in the rain that had started earlier that evening, to see if he could squeeze any more information out of him.

It was busy in the Fisherman's Arms, so it was a while before Bates had stopped rushing to and fro, and Trudgeon was able to find a moment to engage him in conversation.

'Awful night to be out a' sea,' he said, pointing his thumb at the windows that were being lashed with rain. 'Here we are tucked away in the warm, and even as we speak there'll be men hard a' work out there in this weather.'

'Aye,' said Bates.

'I heard two fishin' boats went out from Mousehole yesterday mornin'. They'll be back now, safe an' sound, do you think?'

A young man with a beard who was nursing the dregs of his ale at the far end of the bar was watching Trudgeon, and he chose this moment to call Jim over and order another drink. Then, as he leaned forward to place his money in the landlord's hand, he said in a low voice, 'Watch what you tell 'im, Jim Bates. I don't like him or 'is type. Always up to no good.'

'Is tha' so?' said Jim calmly. He gave the young man his ale, then returned to where Trudgeon was standing leaning on the bar.

'Wha' was tha' you were askin'?' Jim Bates said absent-mindedly, and then, lowering his voice, 'Oh, those Mousehole boats. No, they won't be back till Thursday evening is the plan, I hear.'

Trudgeon looked deep in thought for a moment or two, then in an exaggerated whisper he said, 'I hope it's only fishin' they're doin'. I know for a fact that Cap'n Snipe is patrolling the area, so they'll need to be very careful.'

Bates smiled, then said, 'Don't ee worry, they're Mousehole men and are well aware o' that. You know the score. They won't be landin' anywhere near here – they'll go as far west as they can, away from pryin' eyes.'

'Oh, that's good then,' said Trudgeon. 'Porthcurno, I'm wonderin'? That'd be ideal – customs men don't generally patrol that far.'

'Porthcurno?' said Bates. 'No, that's too close.' He beckoned to Trudgeon, then leaned in towards him and said in a whisper, 'Between you an' me, they'll be landing at Porthgwarra, as far west as they can go.' He pulled back from Trudgeon and busied himself clearing some pitchers from the bar. 'But I've said enough!' he laughed. 'Like the old sayin' goes – them that asks no questions won't be told no lies.'

Trudgeon, keeping as disinterested an expression as he could muster, nodded and replied, 'Aye, tha's for sure.' He could hardly believe his luck – first stumbling upon Sloth the day before, and now getting all the missing information he needed from Bates. Although it was all down of course to his sharp nose, he told himself, and the eye he had for the right person for the right situation. Yes, he'd earned his money good and proper. He'd intended to keep back one of the shillings Snipe had given him, but he leaned across the bar and ordered another pint from Bates. It was still raining after all, and why should he get wet and cold when his work was done?

15

MESSAGES ARE SENT

For the first time, Captain Snipe had been reasonably impressed when he met Trudgeon on Tuesday afternoon at St. Mary's and the beggar man passed on both an estimated arrival time and point of landing for the crew of smugglers. Only a couple of weeks into his job, and Snipe would potentially have Mousehole's free traders locked up by Friday morning: such a quick result was surely bound to impress Sir Fox-Carne.

He gave Trudgeon another crown, then headed straight back up to his office to write a message to the Lord Lieutenant of Cornwall. James Trewidden, Tobias Cass, Tim Newman, Gabriel Madron and Duncan Johns were believed to have left Mousehole on Sunday morning on a smuggling trip, Snipe wrote, and were expected to arrive back in Porthgwarra on Thursday evening. He awaited his orders to lead an operation to intercept the crew, he told Sir Fox-Carne, and was ready and willing to take whatever steps necessary to ensure that these men were caught made an example of, and free trading brought to an end once and for all.

Snipe carefully folded the parchment and gave it to Elijah Critchley, a thin stooped sergeant who had worked at the customs office for many years, and Critchley hurried straight out of the office to deliver it. But he didn't turn onto the road that led directly to Sir Rupert Fox-Carne's house. No, he wove instead along a couple of back streets to the mayor's office, where, walking past the window, he spotted Jonah Gollop at his desk. A slight incline of his head brought Gollop stumbling out into the street to meet him, and as they shook hands, the message was exchanged. Gollop turned away from the street to read it, then shook Critchley's hand once more, carefullreturning it to him. 'Good news, Critchley!' he said. 'Good news.'

While Critchley scuttled on his way to deliver the message to Sir Rupert, Gollop hurried back into the mayor's office, sat down and penned his own letter.

> Sir,
>
> I have this afternoon received good news, which I know will please you. As you foretold, with the trial delayed, Trewidden has resorted to his old ways, and thanks to some diligent sleuthing by the new Captain in the Customs office, Hector Snipe, his latest run looks set to be intercepted and uncovered, this Thursday evening. If, as I hear, Sir Fox-Carne is determined to make an example of Trewidden and his crew, they are likely to face execution, which will set the coast clear for the collapse of your trial, and your reinstatement at Carne Castle. I am pleased beyond words by this news, and add humbly that I remain yours,
>
> In loyalty,
> Jonah Gollop

Gollop sealed and addressed the letter, then slipped back out of the office and down to the grocers' shop that doubled as a post office, on the corner of East Street. He handed it to Mrs Easter, the postmistress, almost bumping into the young Queach girl as he made his way out, and darting irritably around her.

'He's no good, that one,' Mrs Easter said to young Dorcas Queach, who had come in to collect some groceries for her grandmother. 'What's he doing writing to that mayor, after all Pentreath's done, stealing money from poor James Trewidden like that and killing off his mother and father by drowning them at sea when he was just a babe? And if he's not writing to Pentreath, he's sending packages of money to Mrs Gribble, and her husband's no good either. Locked up for that awful business with dear old Mr Coote. He seems to do business with all the bad 'uns, that Gollop.' She waved the letter in her hand, then, tutting, put it in the big post sack. 'Anyway, enough of them. What will your grandmother be needing today, Miss Dorcas?'

———

Up on the northern side of Penzance, Elijah Critchley had reached The Lookout, Sir Rupert Fox-Carne's townhouse, and was quickly shown into the parlour by the butler.

'A message from Captain Snipe, sir,' he said, briskly handing over Snipe's note to Fox-Carne .

Sir Rupert read the message, and turned slowly to Elijah Critchley, with what Critchley noted was a distinct lack of enthusiasm. 'So, it's Trewidden and his crew, is it?' he said with a long sigh.

'Yes, sir,' said Critchley. 'And if they're convicted, I'm sure it will send a message that will reverberate around the whole of West Cornwall.'

'Yes,' said Sir Rupert wearily, 'Yes, I suppose it will. Very well. Please ask Captain Snipe to prepare to intercept the smugglers. I will make my way down to Porthgwarra on Thursday evening and will meet you both at Trethewey Manor, at six. You can keep me updated in the meantime on how the captain wants to conduct things.'

Critchley nodded, then headed back to the customs office, to inform Captain Snipe that he now had Sir Fox-Carne's go-ahead for an operation against the five smugglers of Mousehole.

'Thank you, Critchley,' said Snipe, rubbing his hands together gleefully. 'Full steam ahead, then!'

16

SNIPE GETS READY

Wednesday was a busy day for Captain Hector Snipe. Now that he had all the information he needed, he was determined that Thursday night's operation should go without a hitch. He sent another message back up to Sir Fox-Carne's in the morning, with a request that he be allowed to muster a team of twenty-four armed men, to assemble at Porthgwarra by five o'clock the following evening. Then, taking Elijah Critchley with him, he rode the ten miles out to Porthgwarra, to survey the coast there and decide how and where to station his men.

It was easy to see why Trewidden and his crew had chosen this quiet little corner on the peninsula of Penwith. Here at one of the most southerly points of this part of Cornwall, the coast suddenly pleated inland, creating a narrow, V-shaped bay. At its far end, a steep slipway led up to two deserted cottages, creating the perfect hidden-away landing point for a smuggling operation.

'It'll be difficult for us to lie in wait here without being seen by the smugglers as they arrive, sir,' observed Critchley.

'It will,' said Snipe, his eyes narrowing as his gaze swept slowly across the land in front of him. 'We'll need the men to be on their bellies, lying just over the brow of the headland, ready to rise up the minute they get the word.

70

You and I and one or two others can tuck in behind these vast rocks by the slipway, just up from the high tideline, ready to intercept them as soon as they start unloading.'

'Do you think they'll be using those old cottages to stash their booty?' asked Critchley. 'I can't think there'll be any tunnels out this far west.'

'Almost certainly. They'll want to lie low for a couple of days, and then move it inland when they're sure the coast is clear,' said Snipe. 'Unfortunately for them though, the only place this cargo will be going is to the pound, along with them!' he added.

Once Snipe and Critchley had completed a full survey of the area, looking for any potential escape routes and talking through every possible scenario, they headed back to Penzance. Their horses were weary on the return journey, so it was mid-afternoon by the time they arrived back in town. Snipe met with Sir Fox-Carne to iron out some final details, spent a few hours at his desk planning instructions for provisions that were required, and after only a very short night, was back at the office by seven the next morning to start receiving and briefing the men that had been put at his disposal.

By Thursday lunchtime, Snipe had his twenty-four men, all of whom were armed and provisioned with enough food to keep them going through the night, and even a tot of rum to keep up their spirits. They had also been promised a substantial bonus should everything go to plan and the smugglers be captured – so there was every incentive for them to carry out their duties to the best of their abilities. They ate a little and then slept for an hour or two, before riding across to Porthgwarra. There, they tied their horses up inland in a hidden spot, to be watched over by two of their number.

The men took up their stations along the headland above Porthgwarra, and settled in ready for what might be a long night. Sir Rupert Fox-Carne, as he had promised, came out to meet them at six, and having inspected Snipe's arrangements, he then retreated to Trethewey Manor, the home of his good friend Sir Iain Preece, which was just inland from Porthgwarra cove.

Everything had gone like clockwork so far, and as Snipe and the three men he had chosen to wait with him down by the slipway settled into their hiding place behind some huge rocks, he could hardly contain his excitement. For him, this was the culmination of many years' hard work creeping his way up the greasy pole of the military establishment, and he could not stop himself imagining the glorious promotions and honours that might come.

17

THE FINAL APPROACH

'Are we being met by anyone at the cove, James?' asked Duncan, as the coast of Cornwall loomed ahead out of the darkness at last. It had been a long haul back – three days as James had predicted, and the men were chilled to the bone and exhausted. Everything had gone well, but now the most challenging and dangerous part of the expedition – a safe and secret landing – lay ahead, and on board both boats, the atmosphere was tense and quiet.

'I have no contacts there, and I felt it was best to keep our plans as quiet as possible,' said James. 'Solomon will come with the wagon just before first light to take us back to Mousehole. But no, there will be no light to guide us in. But with the sky clearer now, I think we should find our way fine. In an hour or two we'll be close enough to the coast to be able to work out exactly where we are.'

'And we're storing the booty there, in the cove?'

'That's right. There's a disused cottage there right next to the slipway, with a cellar where we'll be able to store the barrels overnight. It's part of the Penrose estate, so by rights it's mine, or will be before long. Gabriel and I checked it before we left: there's plenty of storage space, and no problem to get in and out. Then I've arranged to have the goods moved inland tomorrow night, if all is clear, once we've rested up.'

'Fine,' said Duncan. 'I reckon we'll be another hour or so, do you think?'

James nodded, straining his eyes to look ahead to the dark headland and searching for any familiar contours.

'It's strange,' said James. 'Planning this trip back home, I felt fine about it. Kept telling Lizzie to stop fussing when she and Joey tried to have me pull out. But now … I don't know, I have a bad feeling, Duncan.'

'That's nerves talking,' said Duncan. 'Like you say, that Snipe character's only just in position. We've got this trip in just in time, I reckon. This little lot'll see you through till the trial, and us through the next few months, and then that's it for you. Your free-trading days over! Isn't that right, James?'

'I hope so,' said James. 'I hope so.'

The two men scanned the dark hulking shape of the coastine in silence for ten minutes or so, while Tobias held the helm. James had anticipated this arrival in the days before the trip, and had expected to feel liberated and relieved. As Duncan said, this was his last run: even if the trial collapsed, Lizzie would never forgive him if he went back on his word and took on another trip. In the past, arriving home from a smuggling run had always been thrilling and satisfying, and somehow, he'd always known, as he saw the coast of Cornwall loom up in the distance, that everything would be fine. But this time, he felt an icy chill of fear.

Duncan suddenly spoke. 'This is it. Over there – that point is just to the east of the beach!' he said. 'We've come in beautiful. Just need to stick close to the coast and we'll see the slipway in forty minutes or so. That Tobias Cass has done us proud!'

'You're right,' said James. 'We're nearly there. We'll come a little closer under sail, then drop the sails and paddle the last stretch.'

Tim and Gabriel, in Tim's boat close behind, followed as Tobias manoeuvred along the coast. He kept a fair way out, but James knew that the sails would be visible in the moonlight now, and if anyone were waiting for them, there was no hope of an unseen approach.

18

*A*T *P*ORTHGWARRA

Time had dragged on, and by gone eleven, Snipe had just started to wonder whether he had perhaps been fed false information by the beggar man Trudgeon, when one of his officers spotted a flash of something lighter coloured some way beyond the coast. He scanned the horizon by telescope, and at last made out the dark shapes of two boats, drifting gently towards the coast and dropping their sails. Word went out among his men, who slid back down onto their bellies over the headland, muskets poised, and for the next twenty minutes or so, a sense of silent anticipation hung in the air. Then, almost at the stroke of midnight, the silhouette of the two boats came into view at last from around the rocky point, their sails down, and the silence of the night broken only by the sound of oars gently splashing through the water.

Snipe had instructed his men to hold off until the boats were ashore and being unloaded by the entire crew, and he watched from his own hiding place for what felt like an eternity as the boats gently drifted towards the slipway and were secured.

There was a pause for a minute or two, perhaps as the crew scanned the coast for any sign of life, and then the five figures began to move in the darkness and take up station, as if participating in a well-rehearsed performance. One remained in the first boat, and the four others stretched out along the slipway. Then, one barrel at a time was handed silently from the boat, and passed rhythmically along the line of men.

Snipe waited until four barrels had passed along the human chain, then he strode forward from behind his hiding place higher up the slipway, and with one accord, the rest of his men all emerged, training their muskets on the five smugglers.

'James Trewidden!' shouted Snipe. 'I am arresting you and your crew in the name of His Majesty King George! Put down any weapons you may have about your person, then each of you slowly raise your hands.'

James and his men froze. They had no weapons to put down – Gabriel Madron and Tim Newman had both insisted on them travelling unarmed – and as James looked into the eager faces of the soldiers who surrounded them, his stomach turned and he cursed himself for having been so determined to carry out this trip, and for ignoring the warnings from Solomon Queach, and from Lizzie and Joey. He had always been a man to trust his instincts, and on this occasion, as they'd neared Porthgwarra, his instincts had told him powerfully that there was danger ahead. Why hadn't he listened to them and turned tail while he still could?

'There's no way out, James!' hissed Duncan.

'I'm so sorry, Duncan,' said James in a low voice. 'This'll be the gallows for us.'

Tobias Cass slowly lowered the barrel he had been holding, and the five of them raised their hands and stood silently. A shot was fired into the air by one of the men, by way of notifying Sir Rupert Fox-Carne that the capture was successful and all was safe, and then Captain Snipe, followed by several armed customs officers, marched down the slipway. Snipe looked triumphant: he had come into this job determined to make his mark, and he had done so in record time.

'What?' he laughed. 'Not even one musket between the lots of you, eh? You must have been feeling very sure of yourselves, Mr Trewidden!'

All the colour had gone from James's face, and he was temporarily speechless, so Duncan interjected quickly, 'Now why would we be needing weapons, Captain? For a simple fishing trip?'

'A fishing trip indeed!' spat Captain Snipe.

'Duncan's right,' said James, taking his friend's lead. 'We are but humble fishermen, we were merely unloading fish caught a few days ago and packed in Falmouth ready for market during a lull in the weather.'

There was a slight commotion as Sir Rupert Fox-Carne arrived at the top of the slipway, squeezed past several of Snipes men, and moved towards the boats.

'Trewidden,' he said as he came to a halt, 'you were warned that we'd not tolerate free trading. So you've been caught in the act of smuggling brandy from France, now?'

'No, we're only unloading fish that we'd caught, Sir Fox-Carne,' said Duncan, stepping forward once more.

But Sir Rupert just glowered, shaking his head. 'Really?' he said, the sarcasm heavy in his voice. 'Break open the casks!' he demanded.

Captain Snipe's men stepped forward under Fox-Carne's order, but Snipe was determined not to have this moment of glory snatched from him. He raised his hand to halt the soldiers, reached out for one of them to pass him a jemmy, and then set about prising open the lid of the first barrel that Tobias Cass had set down on the slipway. He grinned across at James and his men triumphantly, then turned over the barrel, ready to tip out the keg of brandy with his own hands. But what fell, all over his feet and in a great slopping, slapping tumble down onto the slipway, was a mass of long dark brown fish.

'Pilchards!' said Snipe, disgusted and dumbfounded, and for a moment a look crossed his face that made him appear like a full-sized man on the brink of a temper tantrum. Then he glanced around at the crew, standing helplessly, expressionless, and smiled slowly.

'Of course,' he said. 'The first barrel is bound to be the dummy. Critchley, open another!' He passed the jemmy to Critchley, not taking his eyes off James's face, and waited while Critchley struggled to force the barrel open.

'It's, er, pilchards, sir,' said Critchley awkwardly, as the lid came off the second barrel.

Snipe stared incredulously for a moment. 'Open them all!' he shouted, and three more soldiers stepped forward, hauled the remaining barrels off the boats, and began opening each and every one of them, while Critchley prised open the other two on the slipway. There were pilchards in each and every one of them.

There was not one piece of contraband hidden inside: every barrel was packed with pilchards. James Trewidden looked on, trying to hide his astonishment, but when he glanced across at the faces of his crew, he saw something different in them – something more like amusement.

Captain Snipe's face grew redder and redder. He had been humiliated in front of Sir Rupert and all his men, and the smirks on the faces of Trewidden's crew were more than he could bear. When the final barrel had been opened and found packed with pilchards, he kicked it angrily, and it rolled over the edge of the slipway, tipping its contents into the dark water.

'I'm sorry you were brought over here on a wild goose chase, Sir Rupert,' said James, recovering his composure at last. 'Captain Snipe, I'll send the bill for these lost pilchards to your office, and look forward to receiving payment for them promptly.'

Snipe scowled, then began rounding up his men while James and his crew stood by and watched, barrels in disarray around them.

Sir Rupert Fox-Carne called James to one side. 'James, I'll not lie, I would have been sorry to have seen you go to the gallows. But I'm no fool. Somehow you have been fortunate here today. We cannot tolerate free trading, and Captain Snipe is determined to make an example of whomever he can. You'd be well-advised to tread carefully from now on.'

'I will, Sir Rupert,' said James.

Sir Rupert Fox-Carne nodded, then, sighing, headed back up the slipway while Snipe's weary deflated men dragged themselves along the headland to their horses for the long dark ride back to Penzance.

As they disappeared from sight, James turned to his men, hands on hips. 'Right, you lot, will someone –'

But he was interrupted by Duncan, who held a hand up firmly and nodded lightly in the direction of the departing soldiers, to indicate that it wasn't impossible one or two might have stayed behind to eavesdrop on the crew's conversation. 'It's all fine,' he said quietly. 'Let's save what we can of these casks and get them loaded into the cottage. Solomon will be here with the wagon in a couple of hours to collect us, then we can get some sleep and talk everything through tomorrow at the Three Pilchards.'

James nodded. Duncan was right, of course, but he, the crew leader, was confounded by what had happened tonight, and he wasn't sure he'd be able to rest until he knew what exactly had gone on.

19

RENDEZVOUS AT THE THREE PILCHARDS

Joey and Lizzie had been waiting for him when he finally got back to Mousehole, of course. They were curled up trying to sleep by the fire in the bar, and as soon as he came in, they sprang fully awake and ran to him.

'You're safe!' cried Lizzie. 'Thank God!'

'I am,' said James. 'But it has been the strangest of trips. I just don't know –'

'Never mind that,' said Lizzie. 'You're here now, your safe, it's done. And you can tell us all about it tomorrow.'

James nodded. Lying in the back of Solomon's wagon on the way to Mousehole, he and the others had slept fitfully, tossed from side to side on the rough road, but after three days of being alert, and cramped into a cold boat, his body was now ready to succumb to exhaustion. He took his family in his arms, and then followed them up to bed.

None of them stirred until gone midday, so it was one by the time they headed over to The Three Pilchards, and the rest of James's crew, together with Francis, were already there when they arrived. Solomon had shut the inn for the day, and he bolted the door once the Trewiddens had come in, poured them drinks and then came to sit with the six men, Lizzie, Joey and Dorcas, at the long wooden table where they had planned the run just a week earlier.

'So,' said James, 'will someone please tell me what on earth happened last night, and whatever's happened to that brandy I have a huge loan out for?'

'It's all safely stowed in the cellars at St. Hilary, James,' said Francis. 'Just like you'd arranged. But it's over to your lad to explain how that came about. He arranged it all, didn't you, Joey?' said Francis.

Joey flushed slightly, then looked around the table and began.'It was when Dorcas came to tell us what the Blind Fiddler had said, Father. About that Hector Snipe asking questions and getting information from Scratchface Trudgeon. I could see everyone was really worried but you were determined to stick with your plan, and … well, I had an idea.'

'He and young Dorcas here turned up on my doorstep that night and we thrashed it out there and then,' said Francis. 'He's got a good head on his shoulders, that one!'

'Joey,' said James, as the penny began to drop. 'These last few days, when you were supposedly up at your Aunt Sarah's …'

'Well, we had to think quickly. Francis and I went to Roscoff,' said Joey. 'We went in his lugger and we took William Scott with us as an extra hand. We left Saturday morning early, so as to be a day ahead of you. Solomon here gave us the loan of the barrels of pilchards he's had stored in his cellars, and he and Dorcas helped us load the lugger with them on Friday night, up the coast at Bessy's Cove. When we arrived at the Ile de Batz, we explained everything to François-Xavier, and he agreed to give us the barrels of brandy, and to keep the pilchards to pass on to you. We came back into Bessy's Cove Wednesday night, and Solomon and Dorcas were there to meet us. Then we ferried the cargo up to St. Hilary Thursday morning.'

'You went to Roscoff? Just you, Francis and young William Scott?' said James, staggered.

'I know it's not what you'd have wanted, James,' said Francis. 'But Joey's … well, he's a young man now. And everything he was saying to me that night made perfect sense. A lot more sense than you just saying Captain Snipe wouldn't be ready yet to take action against us, to be honest,' he said, and raised an eyebrow.

'Did you know about this?' said James, turning to Lizzie.

'Only after they got back,' said Lizzie. 'I was as stunned as you when I found out.'

There was silence for a moment: James had rested his forehead in his hands, and was staring down at the table. No one was quite sure whether he was about to explode with anger at the idea of his son having made the Channel crossing and exposed himself to so much danger, and Francis and Joey exchanged tense glances, both looking slightly pale. But then James looked up. He shook his head once, twice, and then a wry smile slowly spread across his face. 'Joey Trewidden,' he said, 'I'm proud of you, I really am. And Francis, thank you: for taking care of my son, bringing him home safe and sound, and keeping the rest of us from the gallows.'

84

Duncan banged on the table, and raised his tankard high. 'A toast, everyone! To Joey, William and Francis. For keeping us from the gallows!'

'Joey, William and Francis!' everyone cried.

'It was Sol here, and Dorcas too,' said Joey, grinning from ear to ear. 'We couldn't have done it without them. Dorcas kept watch in Penzance, making sure the Customs officers hadn't got wind of what we were up to.'

'Oh, that was nothing,' said Dorcas. 'Mrs Easter at the post office knows me well, and she hears everything from Captain Snipe's clerk Norris Jones. She knew from him that something big was planned for Thursday, and as soon as she mentioned Porthgwarra, well, we knew they'd taken the bait!'

'The bait?' said James.

'Yes, well "bait" is certainly the right word,' said Francis and chuckled, his eyes sparkling. 'We needed to be sure Snipe would be so taken up with your plans for coming in at Porthgwarra, he wouldn't notice anything going on at Bessy's Cove. I had a little word with dear old Jim Bates from the Fisherman's Arms, and he did a grand job. He passed word on to Casper Sloth and before he knew it, old Scratchface Trudgeon turned up at the tavern, scouting around for information. Which old Jim happily passed on to him, of course.'

'But there's something I still don't understand,' said James, thoughtfully. 'That keg I picked out randomly from

85

our cargo in France … it had brandy in it. François-Xavier opened it and we drank from it while we were there.'

'He switched it over,' said Tim Newman. 'He'd kept back one keg from the cargo he gave to Francis and Joey, because he knows you always like to share one with him. We brought that keg you picked out back to the farmhouse, but François-Xavier stowed it away and brought out the brandy keg.'

'And you all knew about this?' said James. 'But said nothing to me?'

'We knew you'd put a stop to it if we told you before we left,' said Gabriel. 'And then once we'd set off, we knew we still couldn't say anything – you'd have worried endlessly about Joey if we had.'

'Besides,' said Tim Newman with a grin, 'that look on your face when Snipe tipped out a barrel full of pilchards was priceless!'

'Well,' said James, when the laughter had died down, 'I'd like to make another toast. To the best friends a man could ever have – and to a new life without free-trading.'

'A new life!' the group cried, getting to their feet and raising their tankards.

20

DORCAS SHARES SOME NEWS

'Joey,' said Dorcas, 'there's something else I found out when I was in Penzance while you were away.'

The two of them had come out to sit on the sea wall in the thin sunshine that was bathing Mousehole in early-spring warmth that afternoon. The men had all gone home to sleep, apart from Francis, who had headed off to bring his lugger back from Bessy's Cove.

'I saw Jonah Gollop in the post office when I was there,' Dorcas went on, 'and Mrs Easter told me that he writes to Pentreath the mayor in jail.'

'Well, he works in the mayor's office,' said Joey. 'I expect he keeps him up to date with things.'

'Maybe,' said Dorcas. 'But it got me thinking. That morning we heard the gunshot, when we were bringing the lobsters in, and you thought it was a gamekeeper?'

Joey frowned. 'Yes,' he said, 'I thought about it afterwards and realised it was probably that Herbert Gribble doing away with poor old Barnaby Coote.'

'That's exactly what I thought too,' said Dorcas. 'But do you remember, about an hour after we heard the gunshot, we saw Jonah Gollop up on the hillside, throwing something into the gorse?'

Joey turned and looked at her. 'I do remember that, yes. It looked like a telescope. What are you thinking, Dorcas?'

'It was just that when I heard Gollop was writing to Pentreath, I thought, what if it was Gollop who'd murdered Barnaby Coote, and that was the gun we saw him getting rid of up at Point Spaniard?'

'But Herbert Gribble was arrested for Coote's murder,' said Joey. 'He's in jail, serving time for it.'

'Yes, but that was the other thing Mrs Easter said. She told me Gollop sends packages of money to Mrs Gribble, Herbert's wife. And Gribble's only in jail for a year, because he claims he acted in self-defence.'

'So, are you saying you think Gollop is paying Herbert Gribble for pretending that he shot Coote?'

'Yes,' said Dorcas. 'My grandmother told me the Gribbles owe money to just about everyone. Perhaps Herbert Gribble was happy to settle for a year in jail if someone was going to pay him for it.'

'That someone being Pentreath?' said Joey.

'Exactly. Pentreath couldn't have Gollop take the blame for the shooting, because the link with him would be much too obvious, wouldn't it? So, I think they got Gribble to cover for him.'

Joey paused for a moment to absorb what Dorcas was telling him. 'What should we do then?' he said at last.

'Well, we need to tell your father about it,' said Dorcas. 'And if Gollop *was* getting rid of a gun up on Point Spaniard, perhaps we can find it.'

Joey nodded slowly as he put two and two together. 'Because if you're right about this, we might be able to find out what's happened to Aunt Rachel.'

One of the first things James had asked after he woke up that morning had been whether there was any news about Rachel, and his face had fallen at once when Joey and his mother had told him that there was none.

'Exactly,' said Dorcas. 'Let's go and see James now, and decide what to do.'

21

A DISCOVERY AT POINT SPANIARD

And so it was that Solomon Queach and James Trewidden found themselves positioned up on the hillside at Point Spaniard, south west of Mousehole, early the next morning, looking down at Joey and Dorcas, who were heading in Joey's little rowing boat towards the shore.

The wind had picked up, making the sea choppy, and it wasn't easy to manoeuvre the boat into position, but Joey rowed straight towards the rock that resembled a crooked finger, and then tried to resist the inland pull of the tide. It was the same rock they'd drifted so close to that day they'd seen Gollop up on the hillside, and by standing in the little boat, Dorcas was able to signal to the two men as to which way they needed to move to find themselves in roughly the spot Gollop had stood in that day, looking out to sea with a telescope before hurling something down into the gorse.

'Yes!' shouted Dorcas at last, and as the men began fighting their way through the gorse, to explore the area around where they stood, Joey started rowing the boat back out to sea, away from the rocks, to give them a better view of what was going on.

'I can hear the cursing, even from down here,' laughed Joey, as they drifted with the tide, watching the men pick their way carefully through the thick spikey undergrowth.

They seemed to hardly move at all, viewed from down on the water, but Joey and Dorcas knew that they would be thrashing around among the thorns, looking for a flash of metal, and then advancing another step or two to explore another area of the steep hillside.

For half an hour, Joey and Dorcas, in Joey's boat, bobbed around in the water, rowing now and then to keep themselves from drifting too close to the shore, their eyes fixed on the slow movement of James and Solomon through the gorse up above. Then there was a yell from Solomon, and they saw James wading carefully towards where he stood. Both men reached forwards, and Solomon yelled once more, and then raised his arms up above his head. He was holding something that, despite the glare of the morning sunlight shining down on him, was unmistakably a musket.

'You were right!' said Joey, looking up at Dorcas, whose brown eyes were flashing with excitement.

22

A MEETING WITH SIR RUPERT FOX-CARNE

Joey and Dorcas had regrouped with their fathers in Mousehole, and the four of them had then headed straight on from there to Penzance, so by ten o'clock, they were waiting on the doorstep of Sir Rupert Fox-Carne's imposing town residence, with James cradling a big bundle wrapped in oilcloth.

'We need to see Sir Fox-Carne please, urgently,' he said when the butler came to the door. 'It's James Trewidden and Solomon Queach, with our two young ones.'

'Just wait here a moment,' said the butler, showing them into the front room; but he returned almost immediately, and then led them across a big hallway and into an office, where Sir Fox-Carne was sitting at his desk by the window, writing.

'James!' he said, getting up from his seat as the four of them approached his desk. 'I didn't expect to be seeing you so soon. Mr Queach, good to see you too. And these young people are …?'

'This is my son Joey,' said James, 'and that's Solomon's daughter Dorcas.'

'Good day, Joey, and to you, too, Dorcas,' said Sir Fox-Carne, warmly. 'And to what do I owe the pleasure?'

James lay the heavy bundle on Sir Fox-Carne's desk. 'Sir,' he said, 'Joey and Dorcas here were out near Point Spaniard bringing in lobsters for me last Tuesday morning, when they noticed Jonah Gollop acting strangely up on the hillside, and throwing something into the gorse there. He didn't know that anyone was watching, but when Dorcas and Joey told us about it yesterday afternoon, we all agreed to find out what it was the man had been throwing. She and Joey showed us where to look, and myself and Solomon went up and searched in the bushes. We're scratched to pieces, but this is what we found.'

He unwrapped the bundle solemnly, to reveal the long smooth shape of the musket, and Sir Fox-Carne frowned, then put on his gold-rimmed reading glasses and studied it closely.

'I know this musket,' said Sir Fox-Carne, frowning. 'You say you found it up on Point Spaniard, James?'

'That's right, sir. Just this morning. We've come straight here. Young Dorcas realised that last Tuesday was –'

'… the day of Barnaby Coote's murder,' said Sir Fox-Carne. 'Yes, it was.'

He turned to Dorcas. 'And you believe Jonah Gollop threw this musket into the bushes, young lady?'

'Joey and I saw him throw something that day, sir,' said Dorcas. 'But of course we didn't know what it was at the time, in fact, we thought it was a telescope. But when I thought back, we'd heard the gunshot about an hour before, and, well, then I heard some things about Jonah Gollop … and all that made me put two and two together.'

'What things?'

'That he was writing to Mayor Pentreath, sir. And sending money to the wife of the man who's supposed to have killed Coote, Herbert Gribble.'

'This is Pentreath's musket,' said Sir Fox-Carne. 'I'm sure of it. I'd been shooting with him many times, before he was arrested for those terrible crimes against your family, James. It's a distinctive gun, and I'd know it anywhere. Of course, there may be any number of reasons why and how it has ended up in the gorse bushes at Point Spaniard, but I would certainly like to speak to Jonah Gollop about this. It's Saturday, so he won't be at the offices. But he's a Mousehole man, isn't that so?'

'Yes, sir,' said James. 'He lives at Kittiwake Cottage, up on Mousehole Lane.'

Sir Fox-Carne reached forward and rang a shiny brass bell that sat on his desk, and the butler appeared through the door almost at once.

'Barnes, please send two of my men to find Jonah Gollop of Kittiwake Cottage, and bring him here for questioning straight away.'

'Yes, sir,' said the butler, nodding, turning on his heel and heading back out into the hallway.

Sir Fox-Carne reached across his desk to shake hands with James, and then in turn with Solomon Queach, Joey and Dorcas. 'James, I will send you word as soon as I hear anything. Meanwhile, I'd ask you to leave this musket with me. Young Miss Dorcas, you have a clever head on those shoulders. Thank you for being so vigilant.'

23

A SURPRISE MESSENGER

Sir Fox-Carne was true to his word, and sent a message later that very afternoon. But his messenger was not at all the person James had been expecting to bring news from the Lord Lieutenant's office.

'Rachel!' he cried with delight, as the door of the Salty Dog creaked open, and his aunt stepped inside. 'We've been so worried about you! Where have you been? Why didn't you tell us you were going away?'

'I'll explain everything,' said Rachel, wrapping her arms around him, and then around Lizzie and Joey too, who had appeared from the kitchen when they heard James's cries of joy.

'I knew you'd be worried, which is why I came as soon as I could,' Rachel said. 'I'm so glad to see you all!'

They settled together at the big table by the window in the bar, while Lizzie brought drinks; and Rachel took off her shawl and bonnet and then took James's hand in hers.

'I have good news from Sir Rupert, James,' she said. 'Jonah Gollop has confessed to the murder of Barnaby Coote. As soon as he saw the musket, and heard that he'd been seen throwing it into the gorse bushes at Point Spaniard, he broke down, and admitted that he'd been paid by Edward Pentreath to do it. He also confessed that he'd been paying Herbert Gribble, on Pentreath's behalf, to take responsibility for the crime. Pentreath hoped that with Coote out of the way, he'd be acquitted at the trial of the murder of your parents, and the embezzlement of your estate. He had intended to get me out of the way too, but he had no luck there,' said Rachel with a wry smile. 'By the time Gollop arrived at my cottage, I was already gone.'

'You escaped?' said James. 'But how did you know what he was planning?'

'The Blind Fiddler warned me,' said Rachel.

'The Blind Fiddler?' said James and frowned.

'Yes,' she said. 'I had to do some errands in Penzance that Monday, the day before Coote was murdered. When I stopped to give the Fiddler a coin, he grabbed my arm, and said, "Miss Rachel, you're in great danger." He told me he'd heard Jonah Gollop and Herbert Gribble making secret deals, and had seen Jonah Gollop going into Pentreath's house in Penzance the night before and coming out with a big bundle – a gun-shaped bundle.'

'Wait, Rachel,' said Lizzie. 'You say the Blind Fiddler *saw* Jonah Gollop with a bundle? How's that even possible?'

Rachel laughed. 'Oh, the Blind Fiddler isn't really blind!' she said. 'That's how he knows everything that goes on in Penzance. People feel sorry for him and throw him a coin – they think he sees nothing, but in fact he sees everything! When he saw Jonah Gollop with what he thought was a gun, it was the middle of the night, and he was the only one in the street. 'Course, Gollop thought it was no problem if the Blind Fiddler was there! But he was wrong: the Blind Fiddler had it all worked out. He told me he thought Gollop had been plotting with Pentreath against Coote and me, to find a way to get us off the scene for the trial. I laughed it off at first, thinking the Fiddler was cooking it all up in his head, but on the Tuesday morning, first thing, I was just walking through my gate on the way back from buying some milk at the farm when I heard a gunshot nearby. It panicked me, I don't mind telling you. Of course, it could have just been someone out shooting game, and that's probably what anyone would think, hearing a shot like that out there. But what if the Fiddler is right, I said to myself, and here am I alone in my cottage like a sitting duck!

'So, I scooted up onto the cliff above the cottage, on the south side of the bay, tucked myself away behind one of the big rocks up there, and waited. And sure enough, about half an hour after I heard that gunshot, I saw Jonah Gollop coming up my path with a gun. Looking all around him, he was: if anyone had been there, they'd have known for sure that he was acting suspiciously. But of course, there was no one. As you know, James, I always go and fetch my milk at the crack of dawn, and I'm home by seven, so there's never anyone down at my cove by then. Gollop had found out that at seven in the morning I'm always there alone. That was one of the things the Fiddler had heard him asking about – talking to one of the Lamorna villagers, he was, pretending he had some business with me and needing to know when best to catch me at home.'

'So, it must have been Gollop that messed all your things,' said James. 'Looking for you under the bed and in your cupboards, thinking you were hiding!'

'I haven't been home yet,' said Rachel. 'I came straight here from seeing Sir Fox-Carne.'

'So, what did you do next, Aunt Rachel?' asked Joey, captivated by her story.

'I took straight off,' said Rachel. 'I saw Gollop leave the cottage, and head up onto the coast path back towards Mousehole, but I didn't dare go back home in case he was waiting up on the cliffs somewhere, and watching for me. I headed in the opposite direction along the clifftop, then turned inland and walked all the way to Newbridge, to my cousin Mary's. Poor Mary was terrified, and wouldn't let me pass a message back here to anyone: she didn't want a soul to know I was hiding over at her place, and I don't blame her. And once we heard Herbert Gribble had been arrested for poor Barnaby Coote's murder, I knew Jonah Gollop would still be on the loose, and no doubt looking to get me if he could.'

'So how did you know about Gollop being arrested?' James asked.

'You might remember that Mary's husband Isaiah works in the tax office in Penzance, just across the road from the mayor's office. He saw Gollop being taken out by Sir Fox-Carne's men this morning, and word quickly got out that he was being questioned about the murder of Barnaby Coote. Isaiah hurried back home to tell me, and I went with him to see Sir Fox-Carne and tell him my story. By the time I got there, Gollop had already confessed, and had been taken off to Truro. Sir Fox-Carne was just getting ready to send word to you, James, but I said I'd come straight to see you, now it's safe, and offered to give you the news instead.'

'You poor love, hidden away, scared out of your wits!' said Lizzie. 'What would you have done, if Gollop hadn't been arrested?'

'I don't know,' said Rachel. 'Isaiah had wanted me to go to Sir Fox-Carne to begin with, but Mary was sure he wouldn't listen, and that word would get out I was staying with her and we'd all be at risk. I'd thought of just leaving and going home anyway, but she made me promise I wouldn't; and there's no denying that after seeing Gollop leave my cottage with that gun, I wasn't happy to go back there while he was still at large.'

'You could have come here!' said Joey.

Rachel put her arm around him and squeezed his shoulders. 'I couldn't have put you all at risk,' she said. 'And with you being right in Mousehole, there's no question that word would have got out.'

'Surely Gollop and Pentreath would have realised that if Gollop shot you as well as Coote, everyone would know Pentreath was at the root of it?' said James.

'Apparently Gollop told Sir Fox-Carne the plan was to march me at gunpoint up onto the clifftop and have me tumble to my death, so it looked for all the world like I'd taken my own life,' said Rachel. 'They were going to spread the word round that the whole story about Pentreath and your family was cooked up by Coote and me together because we wanted to make money out of the whole affair. And with Coote dead, they were going to claim, I was too scared to testify on my own.'

James shook his head. 'There's just no end to the lengths that Pentreath is prepared to go to, is there? But I'm so relieved that you're safe.'

'We have lots to tell you about too, Aunt Rachel,' said Joey. He couldn't wait to share with her the news of his first ever trip to France, and the story of how he, Dorcas and Francis had saved James and his crew from being caught red-handed one their last and most daring of smuggling runs of all.

'We do,' said James. 'It's been quite a time. Quite a time.'

24

Kemyel Manor

'So now she's back at her cottage in Lamorna, safe and sound,' said Joey. It was Tuesday, three days after Rachel's return, and he and Dorcas had decided to walk up to Kemyel Manor together. Dorcas had been away visiting her grandmother for a couple of days, so although word had reached her of Jonah Gollop's arrest, and she knew that Rachel had been seen safe and sound in Mousehole, she hadn't yet heard the full story of her lucky escape, and Joey had enjoyed regaling her with it as they walked up Raginnis Hill in the March sunshine.

'Poor Rachel,' said Dorcas. 'She must have been terrified.'

'She was,' said Joey. 'And she's very grateful to you, for what you did helping get Lolloping Gollop arrested!'

'Oh, I just happened to see and hear the right things,' said Dorcas modestly.

'Yes, but you were clever to put them all together too,' said Joey. 'I'd completely forgotten about seeing Gollop on the cliffside that day.'

'Well, you've been quite busy organising smuggling trips and sailing the seven seas!' laughed Dorcas as they reached the top of the hill. 'So, is the trial going to go ahead now?'

'Yes,' said Joey. 'They've set a date for the week after next. Sir Rupert told Father that because Jonah Gollop's given evidence against Pentreath now, the trial will really just be a formality. Father's actually going to start work on the renovations this week. He finally believes now that Kemyel Manor really is going to be our home!'

They'd reached the stone gateposts that marked the end of the driveway leading up to the manor.

'I hope you don't take on all sorts of airs and graces when you become lord of the manor, Joey. Father says I'll have to call you "Sir Joseph"!'

'Don't you dare!' said Joey, flashing one of his big grins.

'Seriously though,' said Dorcas thoughtfully, as they rounded the bend in the driveway and the old manor house appeared before them, grand and graceful. 'It will change things. I mean, look at this place!'

'It won't change us. You and me, I mean,' said Joey. 'We've been friends for ever and ever, and we always will be.'

Dorcas's face flushed slightly, and she laughed, suddenly feeling shy.

'I mean it, Dorcas,' said Joey. There was silence for a moment, as they stood before the great old house that was soon to be Joey's home. Neither of them could quite meet each other's gaze. Then Dorcas shook her brown hair off her face, and started galloping towards the side entrance of the house, which led into the gardens.

'Come on!' she called as she briefly turned back towards Joey. 'I want to see the view of the sea from the garden! I need to know where the lord of the manor, Sir Joseph, will spend his time daydreaming!'

And laughing out loud, Joey broke into a run and followed Dorcas as she headed towards the great rolling gardens of Kemyel Manor.

To be continued ...

THE SMUGGLERS OF MOUSEHOLE

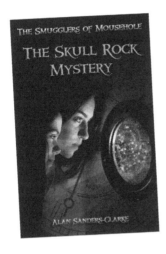

www.thesmugglersofmousehole.com

Other books for adults by the author:

Gallows Tree Hall
(a trilogy, coming soon)

Cornish Short Stories
(coming soon)

Printed in Great Britain
by Amazon

18608614R00064